First published in the United States, Great Britain, Canada, Australia, and
New Zealand in 2010 by North-South Books Inc., an imprint of NordSüd Verlag AG,
CH-8005 Zürich, Switzerland.
Distributed in the United States by North-South Books Inc., New York 10001.

Library of Congress Cataloging-in-Publication Data is available.
Printed in Germany by Grafisches Centrum Cuno GmbH & Co. KG, 39240 Calbe, May 2010.
ISBN: 978-0-7358-2320-4 (trade edition)
1 3 5 7 9 • 10 8 6 4 2

www.northsouth.com

FSC
Mixed Sources
Product group from well-managed
forests and other controlled sources
Cert no. SGS-COC-007065
www.fsc.org
©1996 Forest Stewardship Council

Uncle Rabbit's Busy Visit

by **Christa Kempter**
illustrated by **Frauke Weldin**

NorthSouth
New York / London

"One . . . two . . . three . . ."
Wally was in his vegetable patch counting carrots when suddenly Mae shouted, "Wally! There's a letter for you!" She thrust the letter into Wally's paw.

"Yuck!" said Wally. "This letter is all sticky. Your paws are covered with honey!"

Mae looked over Wally's shoulder as he read,

> Dear Nephew Wally,
>
> It's been ages since I've seen you, so I'm coming to visit. I'll arrive on Monday around noon.
>
> Love,
> Uncle Rabbit

"A visitor!" exclaimed Mae. "Goody! It's always too quiet around here."

"Monday?" said Wally in a sudden panic. "That's today! Quick, Mae! We have to tidy up, and your room looks like a pigpen!"

"Calm down, Wally," Mae grumbled. "I'll go pick it up right now."

At twelve o'clock on the dot, a taxi pulled up and Uncle Rabbit got out, pulling two very large trunks behind him.

"Hello, Nephew!" he called out jovially. "My, haven't you grown!"

Mae pounded down the stairs,

"And who is this enchanting lady?" said Uncle Rabbit.
"Uncle Rabbit, meet Mae," said Wally. "She lives upstairs."
"Allow me to kiss your paw, Madame," said Uncle Rabbit.
Mae grinned from ear to ear.

Uncle Rabbit took a quick tour of the house.

"What old-fashioned wallpaper," he mumbled. "What kind of bunny still has carrot wallpaper in this day and age? And those curtains. Ugh! Well, don't worry, Nephew. We'll soon put everything right. Fortunately I have some lovely silk in my suitcase."

And before Wally could say a word, Uncle Rabbit was sitting at the sewing machine.

"What beautiful silk!" said Mae.

"I like my *old* curtains," said Wally.

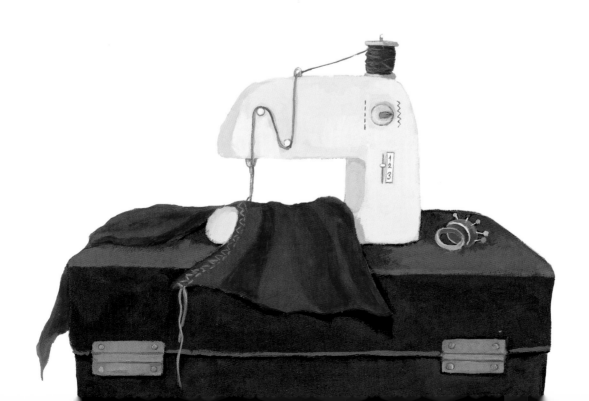

Uncle Rabbit flipped through a large
book: *1000 Ideas for House and Garden.*

He moved furniture.

He made colorful new cushions.

He sprayed rose
air freshener in
the cupboards.

"What smells in my cupboards?" asked Wally.

"Mmmm," said Mae. "That's nice. "Maybe you could
spray some honey air freshener in my closet."

"Anything for you, Madame!" said Uncle Rabbit.

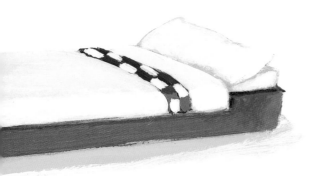

The next morning, Uncle Rabbit was sitting on the roof, hammering.

"What are you doing up there, Uncle?" called Wally.

"I'm putting up a weather vane, dear nephew!
Weather vanes are the latest thing!"

"I like it!" said Mae.

"I liked my house the way it was,"
grumbled Wally.

"I think a short stroll is just what we need after all that work," said Uncle Rabbit. "What do you think, Nephew?"

"A bear of an idea!" said Mae.

"Don't feel like it," said Wally.

Wally stood at the window and watched them go. Mae was singing a song about happy bees. Uncle Rabbit was carrying her honey pot.

"I like your uncle," said Mae the next day.

"I can see that," said Wally.

"Look," said Mae. "He made a bag for my honey pot. Now I can carry it wherever I go."

"So you can make more mess wherever you go," said Wally.

"My, *you're* cranky today," said Mae. "Come on, I'll make us some honey sandwiches."

"Why don't you make some for Uncle Rabbit instead," said Wally, "seeing as how you like him so much!"

Wally shuffled outdoors. He polished the door knocker sadly.

"What's wrong, Wally?" asked Mae.

"I don't like our house anymore," sniffled Wally. "Nothing is how it should be. And you like Uncle Rabbit better than me! I just want everything like it was before."

At that moment, Uncle Rabbit rushed out of the house.

"Look, Nephew! I have a much nicer door knocker in my suitcase. I'll just . . ."

"NO!" shouted Wally. "NO! NO! NO!"

"Why, what's the matter, my dear boy?" said Uncle Rabbit.

"I've had enough, Uncle!" said Wally "*That* is the matter. I want you to stop changing things in my house!"

Uncle Rabbit thought for a minute.

"I see," he finally said. "You don't appreciate my work. I'll just pack my bags and leave."

"Wait!" stuttered Wally. "That's not what I meant. It's just that I *liked* my carrot wallpaper. And the colorful cushions are lovely, but they're too hard to wash. And silk curtains are just too fancy for my little house."

Uncle Rabbit cleaned his spectacles thoughtfully. "Hmmm. Maybe I did go a little too far with my home improvements," he said. "I only wanted to help! Oh, well. I suppose I should be leaving soon anyway. Aunt Betty probably misses me."

"I'm sure she does," said Wally. "And . . . er . . . the weather vane really does look nice on the roof."

Uncle Rabbit called a taxi.
"Good-bye, my dears," he said.
"Next time I'll sort out your garden.
A rabbit can't live on carrots alone,
Nephew! You need a little variety.
Some cabbage. Some lettuce.
Some spinach. I'll take care of
everything!"

"There's no hurry!" called Wally, but Uncle Rabbit was already gone.

"I miss him," grumbled Mae. "He was going to hang a picture for me. The nice one of my five brothers and me."

"I think I might be able to do that for you, Mae," said Wally happily. "Anything for Madame!"